Buster Hunts for Dinosaurs

by Marc Brown

LITTLE, BROWN AND COMPANY

New York ⌁ Boston

Copyright © 2006 by Marc Brown. All rights reserved.

Little, Brown and Company, Time Warner Book Group
1271 Avenue of the Americas, New York, NY 10020 • www.lb-kids.com
First Edition: April 2006
Library of Congress Cataloging-in-Publication Data
Brown, Marc Tolon.
Buster hunts for dinosaurs / by Marc Brown.—1st ed.   p. cm.—(Postcards from Buster)
Companion to the television program *Postcards from Buster*.
Summary: When his father takes him to visit a national park about dinosaurs, Buster sends postcards to
his friends back home telling them what he is learning.
ISBN 0-316-15914-X (hc) — ISBN 0-316-00127-9 (pb)
[1. Dinosaurs—Fiction. 2. Rabbits—Fiction. 3. Postcards--Fiction. 4. Dinosaur National Monument (Colo.
and Utah)—Fiction. 5. Colorado—Fiction. 6. Utah—Fiction.] I. Postcards from Buster (Television program)
II. Title. III. Series: Brown, Marc Tolon. Postcards from Buster. PZ7.B81618Bji 2006 [E]—dc22   2005002590

Printed in the United States of America • PHX • 10 9 8 7 6 5 4 3 2 1

All photos from the *Postcards from Buster* television series courtesy of WGBH Boston and Cookie Jar Entertainment Inc.
in association with Marc Brown Studios.

Do you know what these words MEAN?

claws: an animal's sharp nails

collection (ka-LEK-shun): a group of objects gathered together, such as stamps or coins

discover: to find something for the first tim

expert: somebody who knows a lot about a particular thing

millions: a huge number

monument (MON-yu-ment): a structure that helps us remember an importar person or event

tracks: a set of marks left by an animal that has passed by

Utah (yoo-tah): a state in the western part of the United States

STATEtistics

Utah

- Utah was named for the Native American people called the Utes. It means "people of the mountains."

- The Great Salt Lake is so salty that you can float on it for hours!

- The official state fossil of Utah is the allosaurus.

"Grrrrr!" said Buster. "Rrrroar!"

"What are you doing?"
asked Arthur.

"Getting ready to see dinosaurs,"
Buster explained.
"I want to make sure I fit in."

In Utah,
Buster and his father went to
Dinosaur National Monument.

"This doesn't look like
dinosaur country," said Buster.

"That's true now," said his father.
"But millions of years ago,
Utah was much wetter."

Dear Brain,

Did you know an ocean once covered Utah?

It still has the Great Salt Lake, but that's a lot smaller.

Buster

Alan "The Brain" Powers
22 Oak Stre
Elwood City

"Look at those dinosaur tracks," said Buster.
"They're awfully big."

"But not too fresh, I hope," said his father.

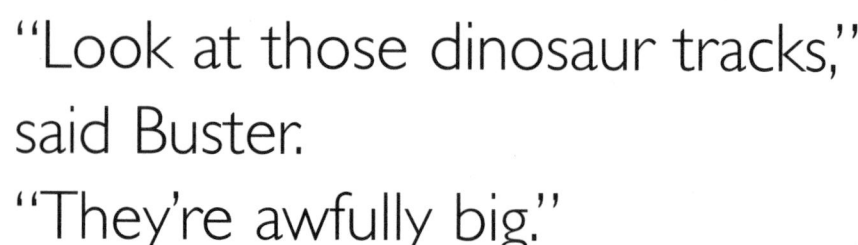

Muffy Cross
432 Valley
Elwood Cit

CAUTION! DINOSAUR CROSSING

DINOSAURS CROSSED THIS AREA 190 TO 200 MILLION YEARS AGO. THEY LEFT THEIR FOOT PRINTS IN THE MUD AND DAMP SAND ON THE SHORELINE OF A SMALL LAKE IN THE MIDDLE OF A DESERT. THEIR TRACKS ARE PRESERVED IN THE ROCKS ACROSS THE BAY.

FROM THESE TRACKS WE LEARN THAT THESE DINOSAURS WERE TRIDACTYL (THREE TOED) AND BIPEDAL (WALKED ON TWO LEGS). THERE ALSO APPEARS TO HAVE BEEN TWO DIFFERENT SPECIES AS THE TRACKS COME IN TWO SIZES. WHICH SPECIES ARE NOT YET KNOWN.

TRACKS ARE SEEN IN VARIOUS STATES OF PRESERVATION, DEPENDING ON THE NATURE AND WATER CONTENT OF THE SANDY SHORE THEY WALKED ON. MANY OF THE TRACKS ARE HARD TO SEE, BUT NUMBER IN THE HUNDREDS. EARLY MORNINGS AND LATE AFTERNOONS ARE BEST TIMES FOR VIEWING.

TURBING, OR REMOVING ROCKS FROM THIS AREA IS PROHIBITED BY L

"Those tracks come from a diplodocus," said Buster. "It was a really tall plant eater."

Dear Francine,

We're going to
Dinosaur National Monument.
I think dinosaurs
would like knowing
we still remember them—
even after 65 million years.

Buster

Francine Frensky
Maple Drive Apt. 5
Elwood City

Buster met David
at the monument.

"Hi, Buster," said David.

"Buster's a big fan of
dinosaurs," said his father.

Dear D.W.,

The monument has over 1,500 dinosaur bones, more than anywhere else in the world. Pal would really like it here.

Buster

D.W. Read
100 Main
Elwood

blue

"This guy looks like a T. rex," said Buster.

"He's actually an allosaurus," said David.
"They lived millions of years before T. rex."

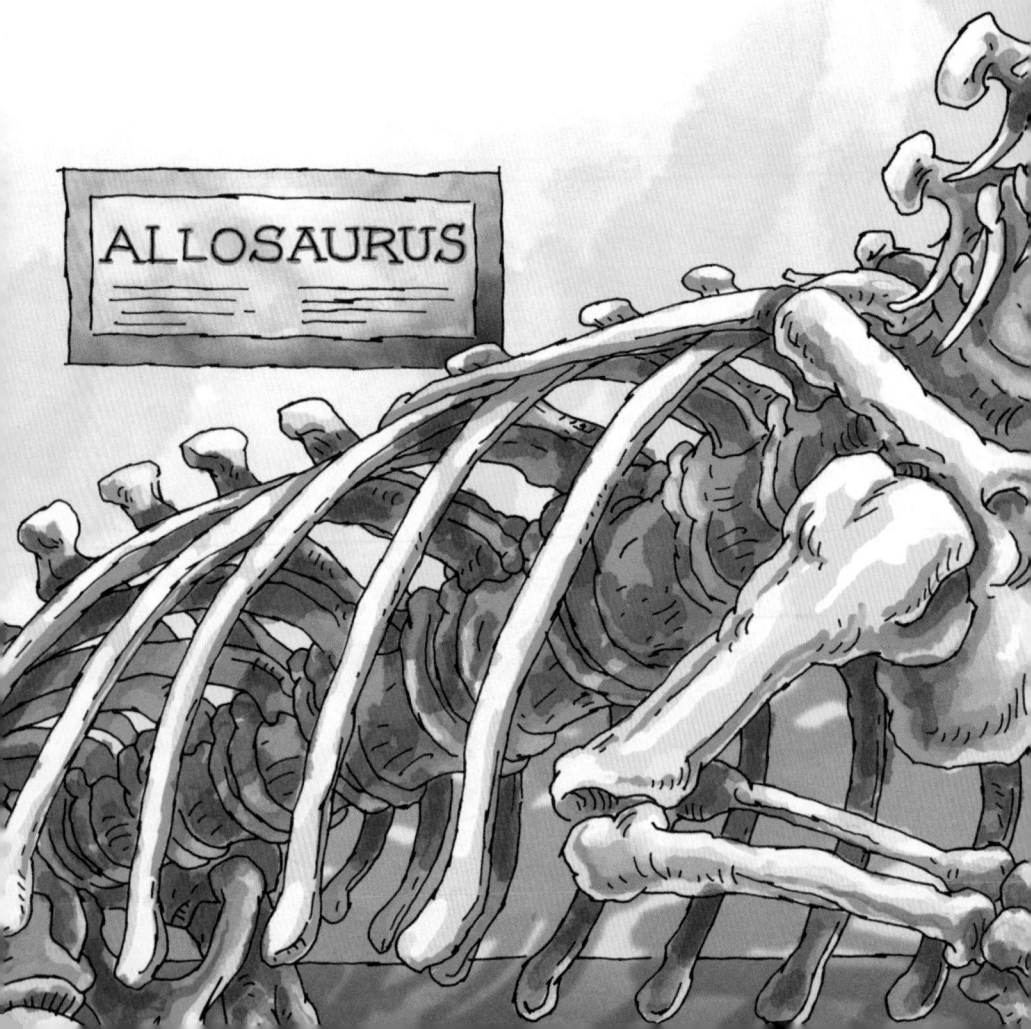

ALLOSAURUS

Dear Mom,

Did you know allosauruses had big teeth and sharp claws? They didn't use forks or knives to eat their dinner.

Buster

Mom Baxter
15 Willow Way
El...

"Buster, maybe one day you'll discover a new kind of dinosaur," said his father.

"Then you would get to name it."

Francine Frensky
Maple Drive Apt. 5
Elwood City

"Buster," said his father, "you sure are a dinosaur expert."

"And after all this walking," said Buster, "I'm as hungry as a dinosaur, too. Let's eat!"

Dear David,

I haven't seen any
dinosaurs back home,
but I'm still looking.
If I find any bones,
I'll start my own
collection!

Buster